This book belongs to:

For Rachel, Elkie and Bronwen
L.M.G.

In memory of my Dad,
who first inspired me to draw
R.S.

First published in 2009
by Meadowside Children's Books
185 Fleet Street, London, EC4A 2HS
www.meadowsidebooks.com



A CIP catalogue record for this book
is available from the British Library
10 9 8 7 6 5 4 3 2 1
Printed in China

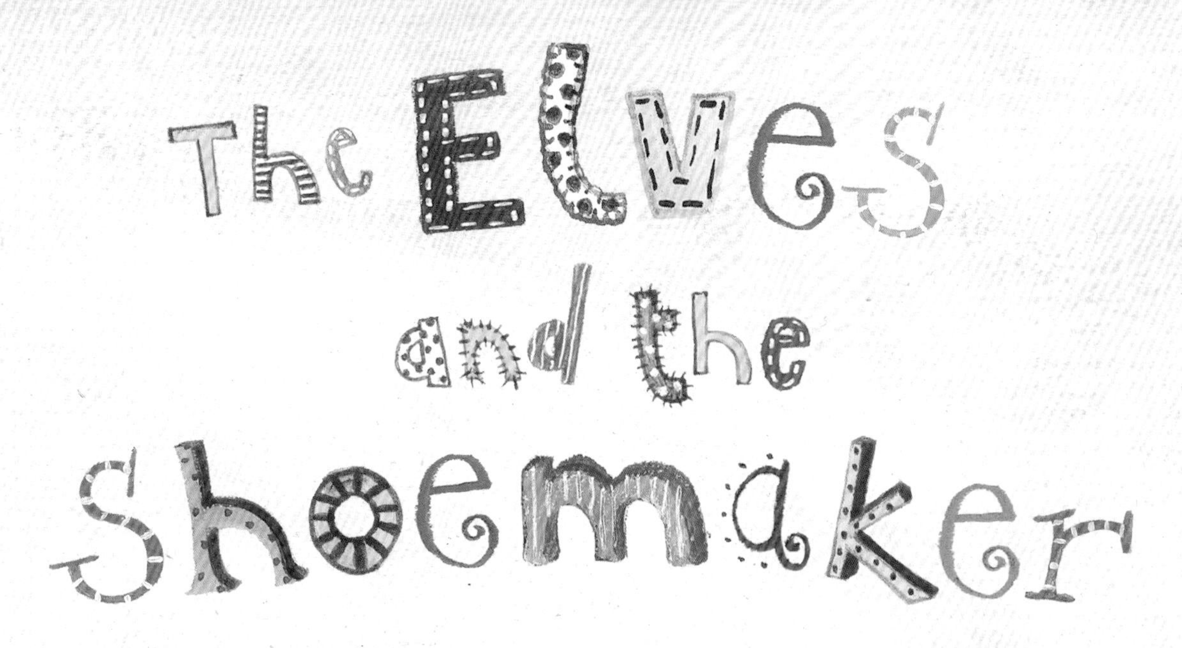


Retold by Lucy M George and illustrated by Rachel Swirles

meadowside
CHILDREN'S BOOKS

There once lived a talented shoemaker. He lived with his wife in a little house, above a little shop, in a little town, above the rolling hills.

From far and wide, people came
to buy their beautiful shoes.

The Shoemaker would spend all day drawing, cutting and stitching, filling the shop with wonderful shoes.

His wife would spend all day helping, searching and choosing, finding the perfect pair of shoes for each customer.

Each person would leave with a pair of shoes that fitted and suited them so perfectly, it was as if the shoes had been made just for them.

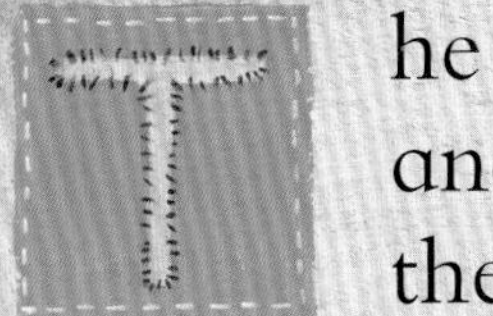

he years passed happily,
and as they passed,
the Shoemaker grew older.

But as he grew older, his fingers did too.
He could no longer work as quickly
as he had once been able to.

Soon, a day came when they sold their last pair of shoes.

The Shoemaker could only afford enough leather to make one last pair.

As the sun was setting,
he carefully laid out
the last of his material.

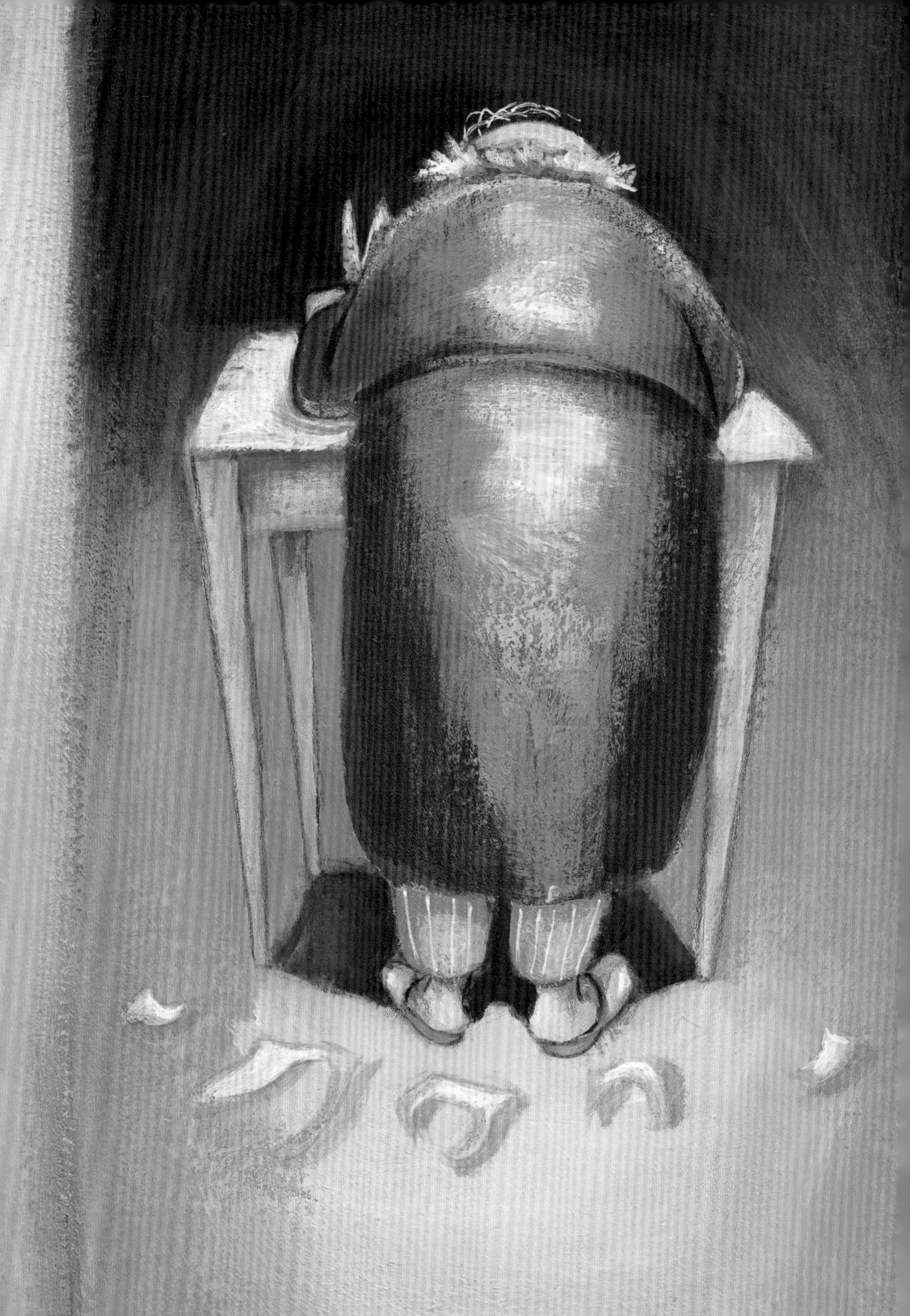

He cut out the pattern,
paying attention to
every last detail.

Then he left the work on his table and blew out his candle.

Together the Shoemaker and his wife climbed to bed with heavy limbs but faithful hearts.

At the crack of dawn,
the Shoemaker got up
and went straight to work.

But the leather had gone!

In it's place, there sat
a pair of beautifully sewn,
immaculately crafted, brand
new shoes. They were flawless.

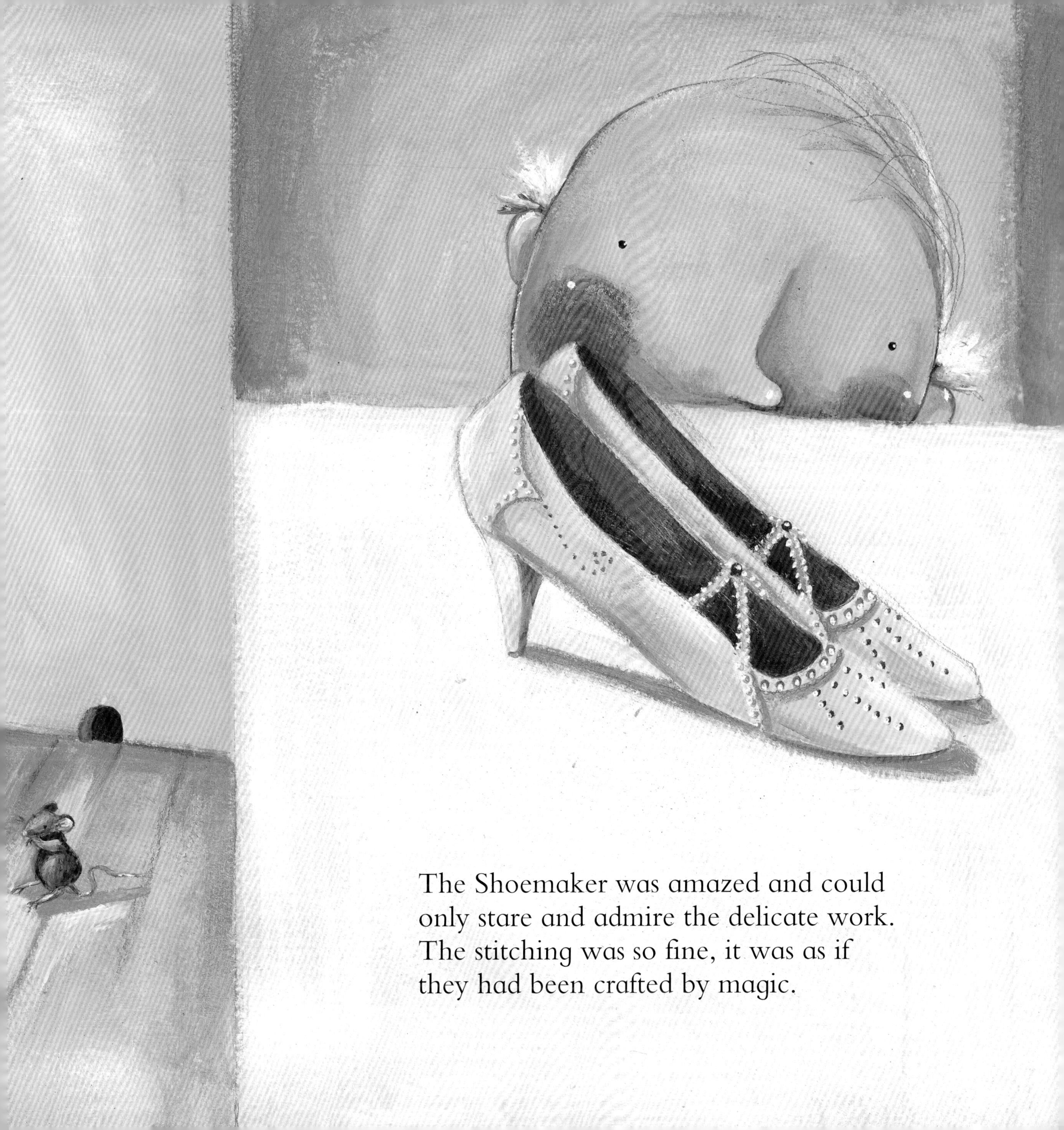

The Shoemaker was amazed and could only stare and admire the delicate work. The stitching was so fine, it was as if they had been crafted by magic.

That day the Shoemaker's wife sold the shoes for twice the price she would normally get. The couple were overjoyed.

The Shoemaker went straight out and bought twice as much leather as the day before. He cut it out and they went to bed feeling encouraged and inspired.

The next morning, the Shoemaker went down to his workshop with a spring in his step.

But when he got there, he was amazed to see not one, but two extraordinary pairs of brand new shoes!

Before lunch time, both pairs had been sold for more than they had ever imagined possible.

The Shoemaker went out and bought enough leather to fill the shop with shoes once more.

And for the rest of the day he carefully cut out the leather.

That night, the Shoemaker and his wife decided to hide and watch. They would wait and discover who it was that was helping them so kindly. They crept behind a curtain and silently waited.

As the clock struck twelve,
they heard the sound of
distant voices singing,
first softly, but getting closer.

Then in the dim light they saw…

…a group of tiny little elves!

They were dressed in
ragged clothes, their tiny feet
completely bare.

With perfect grace and the lightest touch,
the elves seized the leather, the needles
and the thread and stitched and sewed
and worked their nimble little fingers
so quickly it was enchanting.

When all the work was done,
the elves clapped their hands
and sang and danced in a merry circle,
skipping around the shoes with glee.

Such cheerful creatures had never been seen.

Such joyful singing
had never been heard.

Such handsome shoes
had never been made!

There were now enough shoes
to fill the shop again.

The Shoemaker and his wife knew they had to do something to show how grateful they were. Then they had an idea.

They worked all day long, drawing, cutting and sewing...

...until finally,
when the sun had set,
their work was complete.

Late that night
they went back to
their old hiding place
and quietly waited.

As the clock struck twelve,
they saw the elves,
in their ragged old clothes,
dance into the shop.

But when they reached the table,
their singing suddenly stopped
as it was replaced with excited
chatter and squeals of joy.

On the table lay a tiny
little outfit for each of them,

and a pair of shoes
each too!

When they were dressed,
the elves began to sing.
They danced, admired each
other, and giggled and squealed!

How fine they all looked!

The couple watched with smiles
of pride as the elves, still giggling
and dancing, took off into the night.

The shop was flourishing again, filled with beautiful shoes and excited customers...

...and the Shoemaker and his wife lived happily once more!

But from then on,
once in a while, when the
Shoemaker had a little spare
leather and a little spare
time, he would make a pair
of tiny shoes and leave them
out for the elves…

…and sure enough, once in a while, there would be a little surprise on the Shoemaker's table in the morning!